FOR ANNE

Library of Congress Catalog Card No. 85-61398

ISBN 0-382-09155-8

Copyright © 1984 Hodder and Stoughton Ltd
Illustrations copyright © 1984 Martin Ursell
First published 1984

Text by Linda M. Jennings

First published in Great Britain
1984 by Hodder & Stoughton Children's Books.

Adapted and published in the United States
in 1985 by Silver Burdett Company,
Morristown, New Jersey.

Printed in Italy

THE BROTHERS GRIMM

THE MUSICIANS OF BREMEN

Illustrated by
MARTIN URSELL

Text by Linda M. Jennings

SILVER BURDETT
MORRISTOWN, NEW JERSEY

Once upon a time there lived in Germany a miller who owned
an old, gray donkey. For many years the donkey carried
heavy loads of grain and flour to and from the mill, until the day came
when he was too old and too tired to work any longer.
The ungrateful miller decided to have the poor beast destroyed,
but luckily the donkey heard of his plans.

"To be sure I won't stay here to be killed," the donkey
said to himself. "I'll go away to Bremen to become a Town Musician."

So off he went as quickly as his old legs would carry him,
until he stopped by the roadside to speak to a gray-muzzled hound.

"You look sad, my friend," said the donkey.

"With good reason, too," sighed the hound, "for now that I am
too old to hunt my master has no further use for me, and intends
to have me shot."

"Then come with me to Bremen to become a Town Musician," said
the donkey.

"Indeed I will," said the hound eagerly, and the two of them
set off together.

As they traveled on they came across a cat sitting on a wall, and looking very frightened.

"I've just run away from home," explained the cat, "for now that I'm old I like to sit and warm myself by the fireside instead of catching mice, and my mistress plans to destroy me."

"Then you must join us, for we are going to Bremen to become Town Musicians," said the donkey and the dog.

"May I really come too?" said the cat, and jumped down from the wall to join the other two animals.

Presently they came across a rooster, crowing sadly
to himself.

"Cock-a-doodle-do," said the rooster. "I used to wake the farmer
and his wife every morning, but only today I heard that
there're to be visitors coming to lunch tomorrow, and so
they intend to kill and eat me."

"Why stay and be killed when you can come with us to Bremen?"
said the other three animals. "For we are off there
to become Town Musicians."

So the four friends traveled on and on until they came
to a large, dense forest. Darkness was beginning to fall as they
padded along the grassy woodland path, so they stopped at the foot
of a high tree and decided to spend the night there — except for the
rooster, who flew up to the topmost branch.

"Cock-a-doodle-do," he called down to his sleeping companions.
"Over there I see the lighted window of a cottage."

"Well, the shelter of a cottage would be better than the roots of
this old tree," said the cat.

"Who knows, but there might be food and drink there," said the dog.

"Then let's all go there together and see what is to be
found," said the donkey.

The donkey went on ahead of the rest, and standing on his
hindfeet, he peered through the lighted window. Inside he saw a band
of villainous-looking characters, sitting at a table with a huge feast
spread out before them, while against the walls were stacked
sacks and sacks of gold.

"Why, we've stumbled on a den of robbers," cried the donkey.
"And a fine meal they are enjoying, too."

"I could do with some food," sighed the dog, hungrily.

Then the donkey, the dog, the cat and the rooster
all put their heads together and planned how they could frighten the
robbers away and take over the cottage. And they came up with a
wonderful idea. The donkey stood with his forefeet on the windowsill,
the dog climbed onto his shoulders, and the cat stood on the dog's
back.
Finally, the rooster perched on top of the cat, and with one accord
they all began their music.

"Hee-haw," brayed the donkey.
"Yap, yap, yap," barked the dog.
"Meow-ow-ow," yelled the cat, and
"Cock-a-doodle-do," crowed the rooster.

The robbers all jumped up in terror at this terrible noise,
and rushed out of the cottage in panic, thinking that some
dreadful fiend was following fast on their heels.

Once the robber band was out of sight the animals went
into the cottage and quickly finished off all the fine food that was
spread on the table.

After this, each one found a comfortable spot and laid down
to sleep for the rest of the night. The cat lay by the fire,
the dog by the door, the rooster on the branch of a tree,
and the donkey on the straw heap.

Soon after midnight the robbers peered out from the trees
and looked towards their old home.

"It all seems very quiet," said one, "I think the fiend
must have gone away."

"Then I will go back to see if the cottage is safe, shall I?"
said another.

The robber crept stealthily into the cottage and took a candle to
light it at the fire. Seeing the cat's eyes shining in the dark,
he mistook them for live coals, and thrust the candle at them.
The cat immediately lashed out with her sharp claws, and
scratched the robber on the nose.

"Help," he cried, running towards the door, where the dog leaped up
and bit him on the leg. Terrified, the robber ran through the yard
and was promptly kicked by the donkey. The rooster, awakened by
all the noise, immediately began to crow, "Cock-a-doodle-do."

The robber ran as fast as his legs would carry him
back to his friends.

"The cottage is full of the most dreadful things," he cried.
"An old witch by the fireside scratched my face.
As I ran towards the door a man with a knife stabbed me in the leg,
and that is not all. As I ran across the yard a monster
hit me with a club, and as I was coming back into the forest I
heard a judge calling: 'Bring the rascal to me, bring the rascal to me.'
So you can imagine how quickly I ran — and nothing on earth would
tempt me to return there."

As the robbers were now much too frightened to go back
to their hideout, they left it free for the animals, gold and all.
And they ran far, far, away never to return. As for the donkey,
the dog, the cat and the rooster, why they liked their new home so
much that they decided to stay there. They never did see Bremen,
nor did they become Town Musicians, but they all lived happily ever
after in their snug little cottage.